Astrosaurs

THE PLANET OF PERIL

Steve Cole

Illustrated by Woody Fox

RED FOX

THE PLANET OF PERIL
A RED FOX BOOK 978 1 862 30187 0

First published in Great Britain by Red Fox,
an imprint of Random House Children's Books

This edition published 2007

3 5 7 9 10 8 6 4 2

The Random House Group Limited makes every effort to ensure that the
papers used in its books are made from trees that have been legally sourced
from well-managed and credibly certified forests. Our paper procurement
policy can be found at: www.randomhouse.co.uk/paper.htm

Typeset in Bembo Schoolbook by Palimpsest Book Production Limited,
Grangemouth, Stirlingshire

Red Fox Books are published by Random House Children's Books,
61–63 Uxbridge Road, London W5 5SA,
A Random House Group Company

Addresses for companies within The Random House Group Limited can be
found at: www.randomhouse.co.uk/offices.htm

THE RANDOM HOUSE GROUP Limited Reg. No. 954009
www.**kids**at**randomhouse**.co.uk

A CIP catalogue record for this book is available from the British Library.

Printed in the UK by CPI Bookmarque, Croydon, CR0 4TD

For Christian Richards

WARNING!

THINK YOU KNOW ABOUT DINOSAURS?

THINK AGAIN!

The dinosaurs . . .

Big, stupid, lumbering reptiles. Right?

All they did was eat, sleep and roar a bit. Right?

Died out millions of years ago when a big meteor struck the Earth. Right?

Wrong!

The dinosaurs weren't stupid. They may have had small brains, but they used them well. They had big thoughts and big dreams.

By the time the meteor hit, the last dinosaurs had already left Earth for ever. Some breeds had discovered how to travel through space as early as the Triassic period, and were already enjoying a new life among the stars. No one has found evidence of dinosaur technology yet. But the first fossil bones were only unearthed in 1822, and new finds are being made all the time.

The proof is out there, buried in the ground.

And the dinosaurs live on, way out in space, even now. They've settled down in a place they call the Jurassic Quadrant and over the last sixty-five million years they've gone on evolving.

The dinosaurs we'll be meeting are

part of a special group called the Dinosaur Space Service. Their job is to explore space, to go on exciting missions and to fight evil and protect the innocent!

These heroic herbivores are not just dinosaurs.

They are *astrosaurs*!

NOTE: The following story has been translated from secret Dinosaur Space Service records. Earthling dinosaur names are used throughout, although some changes have been made for easy reading. There's even a guide to help you pronounce the dinosaur names on the next page.

TALKING DINOSAUR!

How to say the dinosaur
names in this book . . .

STEGOSAURUS -
STEG-oh-SORE-us

TRICERATOPS -
try-SERRA-tops

IGUANODON -
ig-WA-noh-don

HADROSAUR -
HAD-roh-sore

DIMORPHODON -
die-MORF-oh-don

THE CREW OF THE DSS SAUROPOD

**CAPTAIN
TEGGS STEGOSAUR**

ARX ORANO,
FIRST OFFICER

GIPSY SAURINE,
COMMUNICATIONS
OFFICER

IGGY TOOTH,
CHIEF ENGINEER

Jurassic Quadrant

Ankylos

Steggos

Diplox

INDEPENDENT
DINOSAUR
ALLIANCE

vegetarian sector

Squawk
Major

DSS
UNION OF
PLANETS

PTEROSAURIA

Tri System

Corytho

Lambeos

Iguanos

Aqua Minor

Geldos Cluster

Teerex
Major

Olympus

TYRANNOSAUR
TERRITORIES

carnivore
sector

Raptos

Planet Sixty

THEROPOD EMPIRE

Megalos

Cryptos

vegmeat
zone

(neutral space)

SEA REPTILE
SPACE

Pliosaur
Nurseries

Not to scale

THE
PLANET OF
PERIL

Chapter One

THE MONSTER IN THE DARK

"Next stop, planet Aggadon!" cried
Captain Teggs Stegosaur as he bundled
aboard his space shuttle. A new
adventure was
beginning, and he
could hardly wait.

Teggs was the
captain of the
DSS *Sauropod*, the
fastest ship in the
Dinosaur Space
Service. He and
his crew had been

sent to the Tri System, a colourful
collection of worlds where millions of

triceratops had settled. New planets were being discovered in the Tri System all the time – but sometimes, strange dangers were discovered with them.

That was certainly the case with the planet Aggadon.

Arx, Teggs's second-in-command, squeezed into the shuttle beside him.

He was a triceratops himself, lean and green and very bright. "I hope my niece Abbiz is all right," he said worriedly. "She went to Aggadon to help make it a nicer place for everyone coming to live there – and I haven't heard from her since!"

"She'll be fine, you'll see," said Gipsy, taking her seat behind him. She was a stripy, duck-billed dinosaur in charge of the *Sauropod*'s communications. "She's probably just been busy."

"Probably," agreed Iggy, the ship's engineer. He had popped his head out of a hatch in the ceiling, tangled in wires. "Either that or one of those monsters has got her!"

"Don't be daft, Iggy!" said Teggs crossly. "Of course she hasn't been got by the monsters!"

But secretly, Teggs was as worried as Arx was.

At first sight, Aggadon had seemed a

quiet, peaceful world. That was why so many triceratops wanted to move there. But just a few weeks after the advance group landed, a massive shower of meteorites – rocks in space – had fallen from the sky.

And not long after that, the first mysterious monsters had been spotted.

No one had seen them clearly – they lurked in the planet's deep forests, and their terrifying roars alone were enough to make everyone hide under their beds. Where had the monsters come from and what did they want?

That was what Teggs and his crew had to find out. But since there was nowhere to safely land a ship as big as the *Sauropod*, they were taking one of the shuttles.

"That's the dung boosters plugged in," said Iggy, swinging down from the ceiling. "We'll go faster than ever now!" He cleared his scaly throat. "Sorry, Arx. I didn't mean to upset you before."

"Never mind, Iggy," said Arx kindly. "Let's just get going. The sooner we arrive on Aggadon, the sooner I'll know if Abbiz is all right."

"Stand by for blast off!" ordered Teggs. "Three . . . two . . . one . . . GO!"

The shuttle zoomed away from the safety of the *Sauropod* in a cloud of stinky smoke. Soon the little ship was entering Aggadon's atmosphere.

It was night-time on the planet. An enormous seagreen moon glowed in the sky like a giant lightbulb. Iggy

steered them over grey mountains and deep brown forests until the triceratops' camp came into sight. At the moment it was only a few large huts, halls and caravans. Some of the buildings were only half-built. Others seemed to have fallen down.

"The place looks deserted," said Gipsy.

"Maybe everyone's having their dinner," said Teggs hopefully. He was not only the bravest stegosaurus that ever soared through space, but also the hungriest!

Iggy landed the shuttle in a large clearing in the forest. Arx was the first to come out. "Abbiz?" he called.

"It's your Uncle Arx! Where are you?"

But there was no reply. The camp was as quiet as a whisperfish with headphones.

Teggs clambered out after him, and started munching on a tasty-looking plant growing by his feet. "Gipsy, perhaps you should hoot one of your special 'hello's?"

"Yes, sir." Gipsy was a champion hooter thanks to her hollow head-crest. She took a deep breath and hooted at top volume: "HOOOOOOOO-OOOOOOO-OOOHHHHHH!"

And almost at once, she was answered with a deafening, horrifying roar: "GRRRRR-HHHHHHH-HRRRRRRR!"

Iggy jumped in surprise. "It's a monster!" he cried. "It's come to get us!"

"I saw something move!" said Gipsy breathlessly.

Teggs had seen it too – a towering,

shadowy shape, half-hidden behind a tree. The green moonlight gleamed on a pair of enormous curved fangs . . .

"Change into battle gear, everyone," Teggs ordered. He whirled his bony, spiky tail around over his head like a powerful club. "I'll hold it off." While his crew rushed to obey, Teggs galloped to the edge of the clearing, ready to fight the monster.

But suddenly he heard a high,

bloodcurdling scream from the opposite direction. Teggs spun round. A moment later Arx came charging out of the shuttle at top speed, his combat suit only half on, his battle helmet dangling from his horns.

"That was Abbiz screaming!" the triceratops cried. "She's in trouble. *Come on!*"

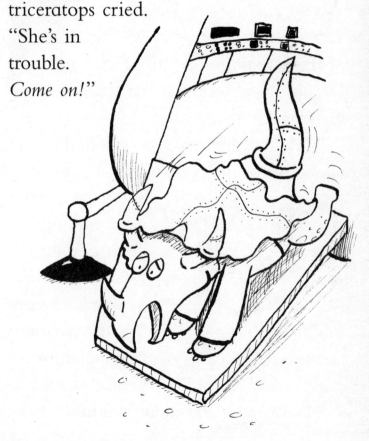

Chapter Two

THE METEORITE MYSTERY

Teggs hurried after Arx in the direction of the scream, trying to catch him up. He had never seen the triceratops move so fast.

"Hold on, Abbiz!" Arx yelled, the back end of his combat suit flapping

 behind him like a funny cape. "I'm coming!" Abbiz screamed again. The noise was coming from behind a long, low building.

12

Putting on their fiercest faces, Arx and Teggs sprinted round the corner. But because Arx's combat suit was only half on, it slipped down around his ankles and tripped him up!

"Whoa!" he cried, and fell head over all four heels. Again and again he somersaulted before crashing into a large tree.

 Teggs winced as a flurry of crimson coconuts fell from the leafy treetops and almost buried Arx. Then he glimpsed a tall, towering creature disappear into the thick shadows of the forest. Teggs started to run after it, but soon gave up. It was already too far away.

"Uncle Arx!" a small pale green triceratops cried, getting up from the grassy floor and dusting off her dress. "You scared off the monster! You saved my life!"

"Abbiz!" Arx shook a coconut from his frilly head. "Thank goodness you're safe!"

Teggs trotted up and knocked away the rest of the coconuts with a sweep of his tail. Arx and Abbiz bumped

14

horns ten times in triceratops greeting.

"Captain Teggs, this is my niece," said Arx proudly.

Abbiz was young and pretty with honey-coloured horns. She shook Teggs's foot politely. "Hello, Captain. I've heard so much about you. I'm glad you're here!"

"Pleased to meet you," said Teggs, itching his back with a tail spike. "What happened?"

"When the monsters started roaring tonight, everyone hid in the dining hall as usual," Abbiz explained. "After a while, I came out to see if the coast was clear. But it wasn't − a big monster was right outside! I . . . I think it was trying to knock down the building!"

Her big eyes filled with pride. "But then Uncle Arx scared it away with his amazing gymnastics display."

Teggs smiled knowingly. "Yes, that was very impressive, Arx."

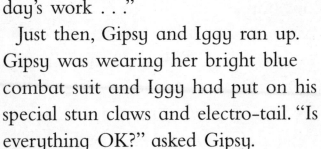

Arx blushed and scratched his horn. "Erm – all in a day's work . . ."

Just then, Gipsy and Iggy ran up. Gipsy was wearing her bright blue combat suit and Iggy had put on his special stun claws and electro-tail. "Is everything OK?" asked Gipsy.

"It is now Uncle Arx is here!" Abbiz beamed.

Arx introduced her to everyone. But Iggy found he couldn't shake hands with Abbiz – he was too busy scratching. "I itch all over!" he complained.

Teggs frowned. "So do I," he said –
just as Arx and Gipsy said it too!

"You've all got *monster's itch*," said
Abbiz gravely, scratching her tummy.
"Whenever the monsters come close,
we're left feeling itchy. Chas thinks
we're allergic to them."

Gipsy itched her snout with her hoof. "Who is Chas?"

But even as she spoke, another triceratops stuck his horns out of the dining hall. He was big and blue, and wore the tall grey hat of a triceratops leader. "Abbiz! I'm glad you're all right, but you really shouldn't have run outside like that."

"*This* is Chas," said Abbiz. "He's in charge around here."

"Aha!" Chas lumbered outside, smiling with relief. "You must be the astrosaurs."

18

Teggs said hello and introduced his crew. "Come inside for some fern stew, all of you – and I'll tell you our unhappy story . . ."

Teggs, Gipsy, Iggy and Arx followed Chas and Abbiz into a large room made from a strange grey rock. Like a school dinner hall it was filled with tables and chairs – and a triceratops was hiding under each and every one!

"Most of my people are timid and shy," Arx explained to Iggy. "They scare very easily."

"But *you* don't, do you, Uncle Arx?" said Abbiz proudly. "One day I want to be an astrosaur, just like you!"

Nervously, all the triceratops crawled out of hiding and returned to their seats. Clanking dinner-bots served up the fern stew. Teggs scoffed his helping in a single gulp before anyone else had even started! Chas produced a small remote control and sent the dinner-bot off to fetch some more.

"They are not proper robots," he explained. "Just bits of junk I threw together." He smiled nervously. "It's a bit of a hobby of mine, making

remote-controlled gadgets. Takes my mind off . . . the monsters."

Teggs smiled as the dinner-bot wobbled back over with another plate. "How many triceratops are staying here?"

"Fifty of us came here to build homes and grow food, so that other triceratops may leave their overcrowded planets and have happy lives," said Chas. "But Aggadon has become a scary place, ever since the night the meteorites fell from the sky."

"I've never known a night like it." Abbiz's tail went all wobbly at the memory. "First the skies went cloudy and dark, blotting out the moon and every single star."

"That must have taken some doing," said Arx. "Aggadon's moon is massive!"

"It was very mysterious," Abbiz agreed. "Then, a few hours later, the black clouds suddenly cleared — and the sky

21

was full of shooting stars!"

"As you know, hundreds of meteorites crashed into the planet," Chas went on.

"The ground shook like a million mammoths were disco-dancing in metal boots. And not long after that, anyone working in the forests started feeling extremely itchy."

Abbiz nodded. "And not long after *that*, the first monsters were spotted . . ."

"Have they actually attacked anyone?" asked Iggy.

"Only the buildings we hide in," said Chas. "They've already knocked down three cabins, two dinner-bots and the toilet block! I myself was lucky to get out alive!"

"Is it coincidence that the monsters appeared just after the meteorite shower?" Gipsy wondered.

Arx looked round at them. "Maybe those space rocks that hit the ground weren't space rocks at all."

Iggy blinked. "Then what were they?"

"Monster spaceships in disguise!" he cried, causing several triceratops nearby to hide back under their chairs.

"Of course," said Teggs. "The monsters

could have travelled here *inside* those lumps of space rock . . . This could be just the beginning of a massive monster invasion!"

Chapter Three

THE SECRET OF THE SLODGE

That night, the astrosaurs kept watch
for monsters around the triceratops'
camp.

"Thank you," said
Chas as he headed
for his hut. "We
shall all sleep
better tonight with
you on guard."

"See you at
breakfast,"
said Teggs.
"Then I think
I'll organize a little
monster hunt!"

A distant, defiant roar echoed out of the forest.

Teggs was aching to try and catch a monster, or at least get a proper look at one. But although the moon was very bright, he knew he couldn't risk a big battle in the dark forest in case his friends got hurt.

The hours ticked by, but the monsters stayed away.

When dawn came, it came quickly. The green moon slipped down behind the mountains. Then the sun rose up like a big pink grapefruit, tossed into the air by a giant.

Soon the triceratops all came out of their homes, yawning and stretching on their way back to the dining hall. Teggs spoke into his communicator: "Anyone spot any monsters? I didn't."

26

"No sightings in the south," said Gipsy.

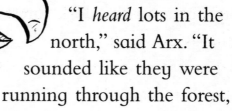

"I *heard* lots in the north," said Arx. "It sounded like they were running through the forest, knocking down trees!"

"It was totally quiet in the west," said Iggy, sounding disappointed. "Didn't see a thing. Not a sausage."

"Well, hopefully we'll see a *veggie* sausage in the dining hall!" Teggs licked his lips. "Meet you there in five minutes – Teggs out."

Soon the astrosaurs were tucking into their breakfast. Abbiz and Chas joined them at their table.

"Here's the plan," Teggs said through a mouthful of fried vines and creepers. "Arx, Gipsy, I want you to find some of these meteorites and study them closely."

"I'll show you the way to the nearest ones," offered Chas.

Teggs nodded, pleased. "Meanwhile, I want the dimorphodon to scan the whole planet to see where the meteorites landed – just in case there's a pattern."

"I'll let them know, sir," said Gipsy, and she quickly twittered into her communicator using the dimorphodon's dino-bird language. They were the *Sauropod*'s flight crew, little flying reptiles who helped work the ship's switches and levers. "They're working on it, Captain!"

"Thanks, Gipsy," said Teggs. "Meanwhile, Iggy, you and I will go looking for the monsters. We'll start in the north – that's where Arx heard them crashing about last night."

"I want to come too!" said Abbiz. "You might get lost."

"We *can't* get lost," Teggs told her, holding up a little red disk. "I'm carrying an astro-tracer. It sends a signal to the tracker on Gipsy's wrist, so she can find me wherever I am."

"But there are bogs and quicksand and swamps and all sorts of horrible things in the northern forest," Abbiz persisted. "You need me to guide you safely through!"

"She's right," said Chas. "Abbiz's job is to make the forest safe before the other triceratops get here."

Teggs smiled. "On second thoughts, maybe a guide *would* be useful!"

"Yay!" cheered Abbiz, bouncing around the breakfast hall.

"Don't worry, Arx," said Iggy. "We'll make sure she's safe."

"And I'll make sure *you're* safe!" Abbiz cried, slapping him happily on the back. "Let's go!"

While Abbiz, Teggs and Iggy travelled north, Gipsy, Arx and Chas headed east to see the nearest meteorite. It looked like a giant lump of green rock sitting in an enormous crater.

"We must take some samples for testing," Arx announced, happily waggling his horns. He was always excited at the thought of running tests on things.

"What's that grey goopy stuff oozing out from underneath the meteorite?" asked Gipsy. "Looks disgusting!"

Chas smiled. "It may *look* disgusting but it's actually very precious. It's called *slodge*, and it's the best building tool in the universe – as well as the rarest. But Aggadon is full of it! There's tons of it underground."

"That's nice," said Gipsy politely. But secretly she thought it was smelly and boring.

"We only discovered it when we started building our camp," Chas told her. "Feel how light it is."

Gipsy picked some up and got a surprise. The slodge felt light as a feather.

"Now roll it into a ball," he suggested.

She rolled it between her hooves – and felt the slodge start to harden.

"Very good," said Chas. "Now throw some at the meteorite."

Gipsy did as she was told – and Arx jumped as the ball of slodge smashed into the

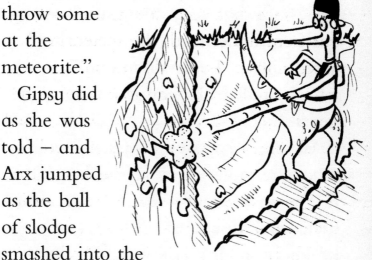

meteorite like a wrecking ball! A large lump cracked off from its stony surface.

"There's your sample, Arx!" Chas beamed.

"That's amazing!" Gipsy declared. "You can use it squidgy like cement, or make it harder than stone."

"And with slodge you can build

anything," Arx agreed. "I only know of two other planets in the whole Jurassic Quadrant where it can be found."

Chas nodded proudly. "Once we've built homes for all the triceratops coming to live here, we shall swap our spare slodge with other worlds, for food and other useful things. There's enough to last us for years and years!"

"Hmm," said Gipsy. "Maybe that's what the monsters want too!"

"Can you show us another meteorite?" asked Arx. "If I take another sample I can compare the two side by side."

"There is a meteorite a mile or so from here," said Chas. "But we'll have to hurry if we want to be back by nightfall. The days are short on Aggadon at this time of year."

The three dinosaurs trudged over rock plains and grassland, stopping now and then to graze. Then at last, on the fringes of a forest, they found another green meteorite. It was twice the size of the first one – as big as a house. Sludgy slodge was splattered all around.

"I'll get you another sample," said Gipsy, scooping up some slodge. She made another, bigger ball and threw it at the meteorite as hard as she could. The slodge hit the giant rock like a bullet. It caused a long, narrow crack to appear. Then the meteorite began to rumble and crumble.

"Look out!" Chas cried, jumping back and clutching his hat. "It's splitting in two – like an egg or something!"

Gipsy's head-crest flushed blue with alarm. "Do you think there *could* be something inside that thing?"

"I don't know," said Arx as the green meteorite cracked open and rock dust flew everywhere. "But I think we're about to find out!"

Chapter Four

CHASED BY MONSTERS!

Gipsy and Arx waited tensely, poised for action, while the rock dust slowly cleared. But the only danger was their having a coughing fit.

"That meteorite is solid rock all the way through," Arx declared. "It only broke open because you hit it so hard!"

"So, these things aren't secret monster ships after all," said Gipsy with relief. "That's *one* mystery solved."

"No, it isn't," said Arx. "Hundreds of meteorites don't just appear out of nowhere – and there were none at all marked on the local space maps. So where did they come from?"

"I don't know." Gipsy thought hard. "They're the same colour as Aggadon's moon. Could they have fallen down from up there?"

Arx shook his head. "If this many meteorites had fallen from the moon, there would be nothing up there in the sky at all!"

"Speaking of the moon, it's coming out now," said Chas. "Night is starting to fall. We had better get back to camp."

"Uh-oh," said Gipsy. "I feel sort of . . . itchy."

Arx started scratching his head-frill. "And me!"

"I'm itchy too." Chas gulped. "Probably just our imagination."

Gipsy gasped and pointed behind them. "We're not imagining *that*!"

A weird animal as tall as a tower was silhouetted against the darkening sky. It was covered in matted black fur. Its head thrashed about on the end

of a long straight neck, and its terrifying fangs curved down like mammoth tusks. Five more monsters, identical in every way, came out of

the forest behind it, screeching and
roaring with rage.

"We can't fight *six* of them!" cried
Gipsy.

"Then let's hope we can outrun
them!" said Arx, scooping up the rock
samples. "Come on!"

And with the roars of the monsters
echoing in their ears, Gipsy and the
two triceratops ran for their lives . . .

Teggs watched the moon float up from behind the mountains like a big green balloon. Its emerald light was brighter than the torch in his battle helmet.

"I've never seen the moon look so large," said Abbiz. "It must be the time of year."

"Lucky for us," said Iggy. "We can still see quite clearly."

"Not that we've found much to see." Teggs sighed. They had been looking for monsters all day. But apart from six sorts of bog and a very smelly swamp, they had found nothing. "I suppose we should head back to camp."

"Oh, can't we keep searching?" asked Abbiz. "The monsters come out at night. We're bound to find one soon!"

Teggs smiled. "You're a very brave triceratops, like your uncle. But I promised to keep you safe. Come on, let's go."

"Hang on, Captain!" hissed Iggy. "Look, there's something over here – stuck in that tree!"

Teggs and Abbiz hurried to join him, then they all investigated together. A big white bucket had been shoved in the tree's bare branches. In the pea-green gloom, Teggs read the writing on the bucket's side:

PERFORMING SPACE FLEAS
PROPERTY OF JOKO'S
INTERGALACTIC CIRCUS
WARNING!
These nocturnal fleas are extra itchy
To prevent escape, do not open container
at night!

"That could explain the itchy feeling whenever the monsters are about," said Abbiz. "They brought space fleas along to distract us while they get busy smashing our buildings!"

"But this says the fleas belong to a circus." Teggs frowned. "Whoever heard of monsters running a circus?"

"What does 'nocturnal' mean?" asked Iggy.

"It means coming out at night and resting during the day," said Abbiz. "Hang on – look!" She pointed to some strange burn marks in the long grass of a nearby clearing. "What are those?"

"They look like they were made by a spaceship," said Teggs.

"A pretty flashy spaceship too," said Iggy, his nose twitching. "Unless I'm very much mistaken, that's six-star dung I can smell – the finest fuel you can get."

"There are funny footprints all around too," Teggs realized. "Some big, some small."

"Shh," said Abbiz. "I think I heard something."

Teggs listened. Something *was* thumping and crashing quickly through the undergrowth towards them.

"This is what we've been waiting for," said Iggy, putting on his stun claws. "The monsters are coming! Now maybe we'll solve this mystery!"

Teggs and Iggy got into combat positions. The crashing footsteps got louder. The undergrowth shook in the eerie sea-green light . . .

And suddenly Arx, Gipsy and Chas came charging out of the bushes at top speed!

"Captain!" gasped Gipsy in surprise.

"Watch out!" cried Teggs, but it was too late – their friends were going too fast to stop. With an "OOF", an "ARGH" and several "OWWW"'s the astrosaurs and dinosaurs collided and fell down together in a tangled heap.

Teggs groaned. "What's going on?"

"Monsters!" panted Chas, removing his horn from Teggs's bellybutton. "Chasing us!"

Iggy pulled his head out of Gipsy's armpit. "Did you see them?"

"We couldn't miss them," said Gipsy, extracting her hoof from Abbiz's ear. "There are six of them right behind us!"

"They're terrifying," whispered Chas through chattering teeth.

"And they are not ordinary monsters," said Arx, slipping a protective arm round Abbiz. "They appear to be . . . *mutant sabre-toothed woolly giraffes!*"

"Giraffes?" Teggs spluttered. He had only ever seen giraffes on wildlife videos. "But I thought they were gentle, quiet, plant-eating animals?"

Arx nodded. "Our super-high-power telescopes show that giraffes evolved on planet Earth – millions of years after we left to avoid that giant rock

47

crashing into the planet. They are
agile, nimble creatures. But this could
be a dangerous, unknown breed that
has managed to master space travel!"

A throaty, threatening roar rang out
through the sea-green forest.

"They're going to get us," panted
Chas, flat-out on the floor. "I can't run
any further."

"You lot hide here and get your
breath back," said Teggs. "Then go
back to the camp. I'll try to lead those
savage sabre-tooths away."

"I'll come with you, Captain," said
Iggy. With a quick wave goodbye, he
and Teggs charged off towards the
sound of roaring.

"Yoo-hoo,
giraffes!" Teggs
shouted. "Catch
us if you can!"
The creatures
roared angrily,

48

and he and Iggy dived off in a new direction through the forest.

"It's working!" Iggy reported, glancing behind him and scratching his tail. "I'm ever so itchy – they must be coming after us!"

"Let's lead them as far from the others as we can," said Teggs.

They raced on into the thickest, tallest part of the forest, where the big moon's light could hardly reach. Then suddenly Iggy cried out and stopped with a jerk. "Oh, no! My stun claws have fallen off!"

Teggs ran back to him. "What's up?"

"Don't come any closer!" gasped Iggy. "I'm stuck in quicksand!"

At once, Teggs skidded to a stop. But it was too late. He found his front two feet had fallen in the thick, gloopy mud, and now he couldn't pull them free.

There was another ferocious roar, and the trees shook behind them. Iggy looked round and gulped. "Captain, we have company!" he said. Six sets of eyes were glaring at them from out of the leafy darkness. "The monsters have found us!"

"And we're just stuck here, helpless." Teggs pulled up on his legs but it was no good. "We're sitting ducks!"

Chapter Five

A SUPER-QUICK GETAWAY!

The mutant sabre-toothed woolly giraffes drew closer. In the dull green light Teggs saw their terrible teeth, their thick, matted hair, their nasty little heads bobbing about on the end of their over-long necks. He tried to dig his back feet into the ground to pull himself clear of the quicksand, but it was no good.

51

One of the monsters reared up and threw itself against a tree. The trunk was bendy and springy. It bent over almost backwards under the monster's savage attack before finally uprooting.

That gave Teggs a desperate idea. He wriggled backwards, stretched his tail out as far as it would go and waved the end about.

Iggy frowned, furiously scratching his back. "Captain, do you need the toilet or something?"

Teggs stretched even further, sweating with the strain, itching all over. "If I can just hook my tail-spike around that tree . . ."

"What good will that do?" cried Iggy. One of the giraffes stepped closer to them, shaking its neck from side to side and growling deeply.

Finally Teggs dug the tip of his tail

into the tree trunk. "Got you!" he gasped. Then, with all his strength, he started to pull back on his tail, bending the tree over towards him. "Hold onto my leg, Iggy. I'm going to try and pull us both free!"

"Too late," Iggy shouted, though he clung on as ordered. "Those mutant giraffes are going to attack!"

Still pulling on the tree with all his strength, Teggs could only watch as the nearest giraffe loomed over them and lowered its head . . .

And a big teardrop fell with a splash onto the end of Teggs's nose!

"It's crying!" Iggy frowned. "What's wrong with it?"

"I don't know," said Teggs, just as baffled. The giraffe stared sadly down at them, gnashing its teeth, its big eyes full of tears. "Who are you?" Teggs asked it. "Why are you invading this world?" But then he felt something tugging on his tail. His front feet started to slide out of the quicksand.

"You're pulling us free, Captain!" cheered Iggy.

"It's the tree, not me!" Teggs realized. He felt like a fish caught on the end of a line. "It's bending back into shape!"

The mutant giraffe blinked as its prey was slowly dragged away by the straightening tree.

"Quick, Iggy, take the astro-tracer from my pocket," said Teggs. "If we fix it to one of those monsters we'll be able to find it again later!"

Iggy grabbed the tracer and threw it at the nearest giraffe. It landed on the monster's woolly back. "Direct hit!"

"Well done, Iggy!" Teggs beamed. "Now you'd better hang on tight, because any moment now—"
BOIIINNNGGG!

The tree sprang up straight. As it did so it hauled the two astrosaurs out of the mud – snatching them away from the mutant giraffes – and shot them into the air like a big leafy catapult!

The two astrosaurs found themselves soaring through the night, flying high over the forest and past the cratered face of the enormous emerald moon.

"Out of the frying pan and into the fire," gasped Teggs.

Iggy nodded, the night air rushing past his ears. "Brace yourself!"

They dropped out of the night sky and landed heavily, not with a thump and *not* into fire – but with a spectacular, spluttering *SPLASH!*

Dazed and confused, Iggy spat out a mouthful of water. "We landed in a giant puddle!" he gurgled. "Lucky for us!"

"But unlucky for the camp," wailed a nearby triceratops, carrying a bucket. "That 'giant puddle' was our water supply. And your crash-landing has just splashed all the water away!"

"Oops." Teggs looked down and realized the triceratops was right. The trickle of water remaining barely came

up to their bottoms. "Sorry," he called,
blushing as he licked up some
pondweed from his uniform.

Teggs and Iggy helped the triceratops
fill his bucket with the little water still
remaining and followed him back to
the camp. Gipsy, Arx, Abbiz and Chas

had just arrived, puffed out from their
scramble through the forest, and Teggs
told them – a little soggily – what had
happened.

"I'm so glad you had a safe
splashdown." Chas sighed. "But it will
take time for the watering hole to
refill. We will have to fetch water from

deeper inside the forest."

Abbiz nodded. "But what if we run into more of those dreadful giraffe things?"

"I think we should take everyone up to the *Sauropod*," Teggs declared. "There is room and water for everyone and you will feel much safer."

"Now I've made the shuttle super-fast, it'll take no time at all," Iggy added.

"Thank you," said Chas gratefully. "I'll tell everyone at once."

"I shall go back to the ship too," said Arx. "I want to study those bits of meteorite – and to see if the dimorphodon have finished marking the spots where they fell, in case there's a pattern." He waggled his horns thoughtfully. "I also want to check my wildlife books for info on sabre-toothed giraffes!"

"Look up Joko's Intergalactic Circus while you're at it," Teggs told him. "I want to know how performing space fleas came to be dumped on Aggadon."

"Yes, Captain," said Arx. "Abbiz, you can help me."

"No!" Abbiz stamped her big foot. "I'm staying here."

"I'm afraid I have to agree, Arx," said Teggs. "You heard what a mess Iggy and I got into. We will need her to guide us through the forest tomorrow morning if we want to catch one of those monsters."

"We haven't had much luck so far." Gipsy sighed.

"Check your tracker, Gipsy," Teggs told her.

Gipsy turned it on – and to her surprise, it beeped noisily. "Hey! I'm getting a signal. What is it?"

"Iggy fixed a tracer on that crying giraffe," Teggs explained. "Tomorrow we will track it down in broad daylight – and get some proper answers!"

Chapter Six

THE SECRET OF THE SABRE-TOOTHS

Iggy spent the night whizzing about in the shuttle. He took the trembling triceratops up to the *Sauropod* in groups of four or five, then zipped back to Aggadon to collect the next lot.

"I feel like I'm running a space taxi!" he declared.

Arx spent the night studying lumps of green rock, and looking for any mentions of sabre-toothed woolly giraffes in his wildlife books. But there were none at all.

As for Joko's Intergalactic Circus, he found that it had gone out of business. Joko spent so long training his animals to do incredible stunts, they hardly ever had time to put on a show! What a shame, thought Arx. Where else could you go to see a spoon-juggling blugbeast, a fire-swallowing ant, super-hoppy fleas – even giraffe acrobats!

He smiled. "I wish we were dealing with acrobatic giraffes instead of nasty, woolly sabre-toothed ones!"

The dimorphodon fluttered about the flight deck, recording where the meteorites had landed and what size they were.

And as the sun came up, Teggs, Gipsy and Abbiz stood alone in the empty camp, ready to track down their mysterious monster, wherever it had gone.

"Look!" said Abbiz. "The moon has normally set by now, but it's still up in the sky."

Teggs frowned. "And it looks even bigger than last night!"

"Never mind that," said Gipsy,

checking the tracker on her wrist. "I'm getting a signal. Our giraffe is about a mile away to the north-east."

Abbiz nodded thoughtfully. "There's a half-built slodge mine over there. Perhaps *that's* where the monsters hide during the day."

"Let's find out," said Teggs.

They moved as quickly as they could, with Abbiz telling them where they could and could not step. The sun and the moon hung together overhead, like eyes in the sky watching them.

Finally they reached the half-finished slodge mine on the far side of the forest. It looked like a dark cave in a rocky hillside.

"The signal is coming from just in here," Gipsy whispered. She slipped Iggy's stun claws onto her hooves.

Teggs fiercely flexed his tail. "Let's go."

"There's a light switch just inside the

cave," said Abbiz, arming herself with a
ball of hardened slodge.

Teggs turned on the lights. And with
a gasp, all three of them realized that
the mutant sabre-toothed woolly giraffe
was *right in front of them*. In fact, the
cave was full of the
weird-looking
animals! But
luckily they
were all fast
asleep and
snoring.

Teggs
advanced
on the
giraffe they
had been
tracking.
"At last,
we can get
a proper look at these things."

"Hang on," murmured Gipsy. "What's

that thing strapped to its back?" She leaned forward and saw it was a small metal box with built-in speakers. "It's a portable stereo! But why?"

"Even savage mutant giraffes have the right to boogie, Gipsy," Teggs reminded her.

"I wonder . . ." She took her headphones from around her neck, plugged them into the giraffe's stereo and then hit play. A terrifying roar boomed into Gipsy's ears, and she jumped in the air. "Captain!" she hissed. "It wasn't the giraffe making those scary noises at all. It was just a recording!" She checked the stereo's controls. "It's on a timer – set to start playing at night-time."

"Hey!" said Abbiz. "When you touched the stereo, the hair on the monster's back seemed to . . . *slip* a bit."

"Perhaps this one is a saggy old mutant giraffe who's lost his voice," said Teggs. "That could explain why he's crying."

"Or perhaps that's not his real skin at all!" Abbiz delicately hooked her horn into a fold in the monster's woolly coat, took a deep breath and pulled. With a loud rip, the wool tore away – to reveal regular orange-and-brown giraffe skin underneath!

"Good grief!" cried Teggs, and Gipsy and Abbiz had to shush him quick. "You'll be telling me those razor-sharp fangs are false next!"

Gipsy gave them a gentle wiggle. "Er . . . they are! They're tied to his real teeth with rubber bands!"

Teggs blinked. "Then . . . this isn't some mutant sabre-toothed woolly giraffe at all. It's an *ordinary* giraffe in disguise!"

Gipsy moved deeper inside the cave to inspect the others. "So is this one . . . and this one . . . There are twenty of them, and they're all the same – made up to look like monsters with recorded roars."

Teggs looked more closely at the one they had exposed. "What are those little red bumps all over his *real* skin? They look like flea bites!" His eyes widened. "Wait a sec! I remember what it said on that empty tub we found.

Extra-itchy circus
fleas – that only
come out at
night!"

"And that's
when the stereos
start playing their
roars!" said Abbiz. She
looked round at the sleeping animals
and lowered her voice. "Do you know
what I think? I think someone landed
a spaceship in the forest and dumped
some ordinary giraffes here. They gave
them fake fangs, wrapped horrid
woolly coats around them and covered
them in fleas that only bite at night."

"How cruel," exclaimed Gipsy.

"So every night, the itching drives
them crazy," Abbiz went on. "And
eating can't be easy when you're
wearing enormous false teeth – they
are probably starving. So *that* must be
driving them crazy too."

"No wonder they go off on the rampage every night," Teggs whispered, his stomach growling in sympathy.

Abbiz nodded. "Meanwhile, those recorded roars make us think they're horrid and scary and out to get us."

"But they are!" Teggs argued. "Er, aren't they? I mean, they did knock over some of your buildings – as well as lots of trees!"

"But what if they were only trying to *scratch their itches*?" said Abbiz breathlessly. "They can't reach with their legs, so they rub themselves

71

against things like trees
and rocks – and our
huts! And they rub so
hard that they
accidentally knock
things over."

Teggs and Gipsy
looked at each other in
amazement.

Then Teggs smiled. "You
can tell who her uncle is,
can't you?"

Gipsy nodded.
"Brains must run
in the family!"

"Noses run
in mine,"
said Teggs.
"And right
now I'm
smelling a
very nasty
plot – a plot

to scare away the triceratops from this planet using these poor, defenceless animals. We must find whoever's behind it and sort them out!"

"In the meantime, let's make these poor giraffes more comfortable," suggested Gipsy. "We'll take off these silly teeth for a start, and dump their flea-ridden woolly coats in the middle of the forest . . ."

Suddenly, Teggs's communicator beeped into life. Arx's voice crackled out: "Captain!"

"Teggs here," said Teggs. "Arx, we've made the most amazing discovery . . ."

"So have I," Arx said grimly. "You had better get back to the *Sauropod*, Captain — right now!"

Chapter Seven

NEW MOON

Teggs made some arrangements, then
went back to the camp. Iggy was
waiting in the shuttle. He had just
unloaded a ton of
insect repellent,
toothpaste and
soothing bite
cream. "Here
you are,
Captain," Iggy
said. "Just
what you
asked for."

   "Thanks,
Iggy," Teggs

replied, climbing aboard. "That should help Gipsy and Abbiz make the giraffes feel better."

Soon they were zooming up through the midday sky. Teggs stared moodily out of the shuttle window. From here, at the edge of the atmosphere where blue sky met dark space, the moon looked silly-big. You could count every crater on its dull green surface.

They parked in the shuttle bay and ran to meet Arx on the flight deck, passing many triceratops along the way. The dimorphodon flapped about them as they entered, saying hello and trying to salute. Chas was waiting there too, and waved in greeting.

But Arx got straight down to business. "The dimorphodon have finished mapping Aggadon to see where every meteorite landed," he announced.

"Did they find a pattern?" Teggs asked.

"No. But they found something else." He nodded to the scanner screen, which was showing hundreds of lumps of rock. "If you were to take every meteorite that fell and put them all back together, you would be left with a massive lump of rock. A lump of rock exactly the same size, shape and colour as Aggadon's moon."

Teggs and Iggy swapped incredulous looks, and Chas seemed totally flabbergasted.

"I also studied the rock samples," Arx went on. "I know it sounds crazy, but the evidence says those meteorites are all that's left of Aggadon's moon after some terrible catastrophe tore it apart!"

"But the moon is still in the sky," Iggy protested. "You can't miss it — it's big enough!"

"And getting bigger all the time,"

77

Teggs said slowly. "What's going on, Arx?"

Arx paused. "I have a theory. But it's wilder than a T. rex pyjama party! Chas, you said that on the night of the  meteorites it went very, very dark."

Chas nodded. "The moon and the stars were blotted out by dark clouds."

"Or dark *smoke*," said Arx. "A *smokescreen*! I think someone blotted out the sky so they could blow up the moon and replace it with a replica without anyone noticing."

"*What?*" squeaked Chas, clutching his hat.

"Of course!" said Teggs. "They must have used the same smokescreen to keep them hidden while they took the giraffes down to the planet in their spaceship. Harmless giraffes, made to

look and act like monsters in the hope
of scaring everyone away!"

"*Harmless* giraffes?" gibbered Chas, his
brain boggling.

"But why?" wondered Iggy. "And if
the moon *has* blown up, what's that in
the sky over Aggadon now? How come
it's growing bigger every night?"

"It isn't growing bigger," said Arx
gravely. "It's getting *closer*. It's
approaching Aggadon at a hundred

miles per hour, and picking up speed
all the time."

Teggs jumped into his control pit. "I
think it's time we took a closer look at
this so-called moon. Let's go!"

The dimorphodon started bashing
buttons with their beaks and twisting
dials with their claws. The *Sauropod*
throbbed with power as Arx steered a
course for the mysterious moon. Teggs
saw it on the scanner, like a big green
snooker ball.

Suddenly a sleek, sinister spaceship
shot out from behind it – and
fired lasers at point-blank
range!

"Raise the shields!"
bellowed Teggs –
but too late.
The lasers
tore into
the
Sauropod.

The mighty ship shook and spun under the surprise attack. Chas clung on to Gipsy's empty chair for dear life.

"Red alert!" screeched the alarm pterosaur. "Battle stations! Man the lifeboats! *Squawwwwk!*"

"Our power banks have been hit," Arx gasped. "There's not enough energy for our shields."

"Launch the dung torpedoes," Teggs shouted.

"Not enough power for those either!" cried Iggy.

"They're firing again!" said Arx. The ship rocked and rattled as the blasts hit home. "They've blown a hole right through to level nine, and they're bringing their ship in closer." The lights dipped down to a warning red as Arx peered at his instruments. "Captain, whoever's attacking us . . . I think they're coming aboard!"

Chapter Eight

THE WRECKING CREW

Teggs leaped out of the control pit. "Arx, send all ankylosaur guards to level nine," he snapped. "We're not giving up without a fight!"

"I'm with you, Captain," said Iggy, and the two of them ran to the lift.

"Prepare for battle!" The alarm pterosaur's squawk echoed around the ship. "Intruders on board! Big,

fat, hairy intruders on board!"

"They'll be small, sad, floppy intruders by the time I'm finished with them!" said Iggy fiercely as the lift whooshed them downwards. "Captain, I recognized their ship. It's a Dungdozer Prime – which runs on six-star dung."

"Then it's the same ship that brought the giraffes to Aggadon," Teggs realized. "And the space-circus fleas too. We're about to meet the masterminds behind this plan."

"Masterminds? They must be stupid to come aboard on level nine!" Iggy laughed. "They'll have to fight their way through eight whole levels to get to the flight deck."

"Maybe they don't *want* to reach the flight deck!" Teggs gasped. "The engines are on level nine! What if they are after those?"

"My lovely engines?" Iggy turned crimson with rage. "Let's get fighting!"

The lift doors opened and Teggs and Iggy burst out onto level nine, following the sounds of battle. They passed a few panicking triceratops and a pterodactyl cleaner hiding (very badly) in a bucket. But then, to their dismay, they found that the ankylosaur guards were in retreat.

"What's happening?" Teggs asked Alass, the security chief.

"They've got quick-drying cement shooters!" she gasped, her knobbly back covered in white splatters. "They've stuck my boys' feet to the floor."

"They've got gravel cannons too!" groaned another ankylosaur.

"And concrete-dust grenades," coughed another.

"*Who* has got all these things?" Teggs demanded.

"*They* have!" Iggy pointed as four large, shambling creatures came round the corner. "Mammoth builders!"

Teggs's eyes narrowed at the sight of them. He had met mammoths before, and knew they meant big trouble. They looked like brutish elephants covered in thick woolly hair and wearing hard hats. Strange, scruffy tools and weapons

were strapped to their backs. But while
most mammoths had long curving
tusks, this group had none at all.

"We're not just builders," said the
leading mammoth. "My name's Tonka,
and this is my wrecking crew. We will
demolish your engine room unless you
surrender right now!"

"I say we fight 'em, Captain!"
snarled Iggy, charging forward.

Teggs whipped out his tail and
dragged Iggy back. "Without the

engines we will be totally helpless," he reminded the incensed iguanodon. "I think we should hear what they have to say." He looked up at Tonka. "But first, prove to me the engines aren't *already* demolished!"

Tonka smiled nastily. "All right. Send away your useless guards and let's have a little chat in the engine room."

Teggs and Iggy followed them down the corridor. They passed ankylosaurs stuck in concrete puddles and lying dazed in clouds of dust. "Don't worry," Teggs told them kindly. "It will be all right."

Tonka sniggered. "That's what *you* think."

He and his wrecking crew swaggered into the engine room. Two more mammoths were waiting inside, one big, one small. They swigged hot sweet tea from dirty cups while leaning on picks and shovels. But as Teggs and Iggy came in, the big one grabbed a cement shooter with his trunk and aimed it straight at them.

"Did you do the job, Marvin?" Tonka asked.

The mammoth with the cannon nodded. "Yup."

"What are you up to?" Teggs demanded. "Why did you attack us like this?"

"Because we don't want you sticking your beaks into our business!" snarled Tonka, gulping down a big mug of tea and stuffing his mouth with biscuits. "Our plan to scare the triceratops away worked a treat. You even took them off the planet for us.

And if you had just pushed off into outer space like good little astrosaurs, you wouldn't be in such trouble now."

"Yeah, yeah, whatever," said Teggs. "Just tell me – why are you doing all this?"

Tonka went all dreamy-eyed. "Because Aggadon is stuffed full of slodge, that's why."

Iggy blinked. "What, that gloopy grey stuff?"

"It's a builder's dream!" said Tonka. "The super-duper, super-rare super-cement."

"And it's super-expensive too," chirped Marvin. "There's enough there to make us *ultra*-rich!"

"We'd give our tusks for a treasure like that," agreed his mate.

"We *did* give our tusks for it!" Tonka reminded them. "We broke them off and gave them to the giraffes to wear as false teeth. Like we shaved our tummies to dress them up in woolly coats!" He reared up to show off his pink billowing belly.

"Why bother to dress up some giraffes?" asked Iggy. "Why not use real monsters?"

"I'll bet they were too scared," Teggs jeered.

"It wasn't just that," Tonka argued. "Er, I mean, it

92

wasn't that at all! Thing was, we'd just finished bulldozing an old space circus and some giraffes had been left behind, together with a few performing fleas."

Iggy frowned. "What were giraffes doing in a circus?"

"They were trained to be famous acrobats," said Tonka. "But the circus shut down before they had a chance to perform." His trunk trembled with a sinister snigger. "Well, they've performed for *us* all right! We dressed 'em up, set loose the fleas, recorded some roars and hey presto — instant scary monsters!"

"You are cruel and horrible," said Teggs

93

sternly. "But why did you even have to scare the triceratops away? There's only fifty of them, you could have just started mining slodge on the rest of the planet without them knowing."

"But we aren't miners, are we?" Tonka grinned nastily. "We're *wreckers*. Mining all the slodge would take years and years – so instead we're going to smash up the whole planet! We'll wreck it to rubble and suck up all the slodge with space-hoovers. Then we can build with it all over the Jurassic Quadrant!"

Iggy scoffed. "You can't just wreck a whole planet!"

"You can when you've got a big remote-controlled wrecking ball," said Tonka, his piggy little eyes sparkling. "A wrecking ball the size of a *moon!*"

"Oh, *no*," Teggs groaned. "*That's* why they sneakily switched Aggadon's moon. All this time we've been looking up at a giant wrecking ball – swinging closer to the planet with every passing second!"

Iggy buried his head in his claws. "And Gipsy and Abbiz are stranded down there!"

95

Chapter Nine

THE LEAVING PRESENT

Teggs glared at
the smug
mammoths.
"You'll never
get away with
this, you
tuskless tricksters!
The DSS will
hunt you down
and make you pay."

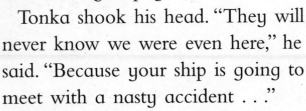

Tonka shook his head. "They will
never know we were even here," he
said. "Because your ship is going to
meet with a nasty accident . . ."

"Since we can't scare you away,

we're going to have to squish you,"
explained Marvin, sucking more tea up
his trunk. "We can't let anything get in
the way of our profits!"

Just then, someone cheeped from the
engine room's doorway. It was the
leader of the
dimorphodon, a
plucky little
dino-bird
named Sprite.
He winked at
Teggs.

Marvin tilted
his trunk.
"What's that
thing?"

"Er, just
one of my
pet parakeets,"
said Teggs
quickly.

"*Eep!*" Another of the dimorphodon fluttered into the room, closely followed by another.

"Sweet! Maybe we'll take them with us before we wreck your ship!" Tonka gave a soppy smile as Sprite flapped over and perched on his head. "Who's an ickle-wickle birdie then?"

"*Ch-ch-ch-ch*," said Sprite happily. And then he gave Tonka a whopping great peck, right on the tip of his trunk!

"Owwwwww!" trumpeted Tonka.

"*Nowwwww!*" shouted Teggs.

At their captain's signal, a whole flock of dimorphodon flew into the room. They flapped about the mammoths, tugging on their woolly hair and snapping at their floppy ears. At the same time, Iggy jumped on Tonka while Teggs charged at Marvin. The mammoth fired his cement shooter, but Teggs leaped through the air and the quick-drying paste landed harmlessly on the floor. Then Teggs gave the mammoth a whack on the back, crushing his collection of weapons.

"Come on, lads, let's get out of here!"
cried Tonka, shaking Iggy off his leg.
His mammoth wrecking crew were
already speeding for the exit, ears
pressed down against their heads and
trunks rolled up tight as the
dimorphodon hit them on the bottom
with their own shovels.

Teggs and Iggy threw Marvin after
them. "Don't forget to take your
rubbish home with you!"

Marvin landed with a mammoth
thud. Tonka crossly helped him up.
"You haven't won, Captain," he
snarled. "You'll see!" Then they both

vanished through the door.

"Iggy, take the dimorphodon and Alass and get after them," said Teggs. "I've got to get to Aggadon and rescue Gipsy and Abbiz!"

"Yes, sir." Iggy saluted and charged off with Sprite and his flock.

Teggs galloped off to the lift and returned to the flight deck, where Arx and Chas were working at the controls. "Thanks for sending the dimorphodon down to help us!" he said.

"I was listening in to your conversation," Arx explained. "And don't worry, I'm already taking the *Sauropod* back into Aggadon's orbit."

Chas nodded. "We *must* get Abbiz and Gipsy back safely."

"Is there any way we can stop that wrecking-ball moon?" asked Teggs.

"There's just one chance," said Arx. "The mammoths are steering it by

 remote control. If we can only make a *stronger* remote control, we can steer away the moon harmlessly into deep space."

"Can you do that, Arx?" Teggs asked hopefully.

"No," Arx admitted. Then he patted Chas proudly. "But luckily Chas here is a remote-control expert, remember?"

"Of course!" exclaimed Teggs, remembering the remote-controlled dinner-bots in the camp canteen.

"I'm on the case," Chas promised, holding up a homemade gadget with wires hanging out. "Working as fast as I can!"

Just then, the alarm pterosaur gave a piercing squawk. "Intruders retreating! Mammoths pushing off!"

"They gave up very easily." Teggs frowned. "They had *us* on the run before."

But suddenly the *Sauropod* went *BOOM!* It shook like a star had gone supernova at its centre. Teggs staggered about as the ship started to spiral and spin and alarms went off everywhere. "What's happening?"

Iggy's heartbroken face appeared on the scanner screen. "Those evil mammoths must have hidden a gravel-grenade in the engine room, set on a timer. Now it's gone off and demolished the engines!"

"No wonder they were in a hurry to get back to their ship," Teggs realized. "Can you fix the damage, Iggy?"

"It'll take ages," said Iggy. "And we don't *have* ages. Without engines, we'll start falling out of the sky!"

Teggs felt his stomach lurch as the *Sauropod* started to dip.

"Iggy is right," Arx shouted. "If we don't land on Aggadon soon, we will *crash* into it! I'm losing control!"

Chas almost ate his own hat with fear. Just then, the lift doors swooshed open and the dimorphodon flew back inside. They went straight to their stations to help Arx land the stricken *Sauropod*.

Teggs gave a crooked smile. They hadn't given up yet, and neither would he. As the ship zoomed wonkily down to the planet's surface, he staggered over to Gipsy's loudspeaker. "Attention, crew!" he shouted. "Hold on tight. This landing is going to be a bit bumpy!" The dimorphodon couldn't keep the ship in the air a moment longer. *WHAM!* It dropped like a stone, deep in the overgrown heart of a far-reaching forest. Trunks splintered. Leaves exploded into the air like confetti.

But the *Sauropod* landed in one piece!

The sound of cheering all over the ship carried up to the flight deck. The dimorphodon clapped their wings and whistled a joyful tune.

But then a woolly face with a long rubbery trunk zapped into sight on the scanner.

"Tonka!" snarled Teggs. "You sneaky ship-scuttler, what do you want now?"

"I'm so glad you landed safely, Captain," said Tonka, slurping tea from a large bucket. "You see, I'm very proud of my remote-controlled

wrecking-ball moon, but I've had to keep it secret. Now you, your crew and your rotten little parakeets can admire it for yourselves – close up!" He sniggered. "That moon will come crashing down on your heads in precisely *ten* minutes. You will be squished, Aggadon will be crushed, we'll suck up the slodge and be on our way." He waved at them with his trunk. "Enjoy your last moments, astro-fools. This time there is no escape!"

Chapter Ten

REMOTE *OUT-OF*-CONTROL!

"We're not beaten yet," cried Teggs as the scanner went dark. "Chas, how's your special remote-control thingie coming along?"

Chas was working furiously. "There! It's finished."

"Then let's get outside," said Teggs, hooking his tail round Chas and dragging him into the lift. "Quick!"

Together with Arx, they ran to the ship's main hatchway, picking up Iggy on the way. Once there, to Teggs's delight he saw two familiar faces waiting to greet him – and an awful lot of giraffes.

"Gipsy! Abbiz!" he cried. "It's great to see you."

There were quick hugs all round.

"We were feeding the giraffes in the forest when we saw you make a forced landing," Gipsy explained.

"We came running. What's going on?"

"And what has happened to the moon?" asked Abbiz, pointing up at the sky.

Teggs turned, and a spine-chilling tingle ran through every armoured plate on his back. The moon very nearly filled the whole sky. It looked like a giant glowing green bowling ball about to flatten them.

"The mammoths are behind everything," Teggs explained. "That moon is really a remote-controlled wrecking ball. And only Chas can stop it."

112

Chas switched on his strange device. "I hope to send a more powerful remote-control signal that will let me steer away the runaway moon." He pulled out the aerial. "Here goes!"

Everyone watched as he switched on the device and pointed it at the wrecking ball.

But nothing happened!

"Is it broken?" asked Gipsy.

"I don't think so." Chas groaned. "It must be these tall trees all around us, blocking the signal!"

"There are only five minutes left before the moon hits!" cried Teggs. "We must get out of this forest, and fast!"

"That will take ten minutes at least," said Abbiz quietly. "We'll never make it."

"Then I guess it's all over." Arx sighed, hugging Abbiz close. "The mammoths win after all."

Everyone waited in tense, helpless silence as the moon loomed ever-larger overhead.

"It's the giraffes I really feel sorry for," said Iggy unexpectedly. "First they were abandoned by the space circus. Then they were kidnapped and dressed up. Now they're going to be squashed flat by a mammoth moon. What rotten luck!"

"Space circus?" Gipsy frowned. "Whatever would giraffes be doing in a space circus?"

"Acrobatics, apparently," said Arx.

"According to space records, Joko – the owner of the circus – was a genius at training all kinds of animals . . ."

Then, even as he spoke, six of the giraffes grouped together in a line, so that five more could jump on their backs! The dinosaurs gasped as four more giraffes scrambled up onto *their* backs. And then three more did the same . . .

"Bless my horns!" said Arx. "They really *are* acrobatic giraffes. Joko *was* a genius. Look, they're making a giraffe pyramid!"

Iggy led a round of applause. "Show us another trick!"

"Wait!" Teggs shouted. "Don't you see? The giraffes at the top are taller than the trees! If we could only work the remote control from up there, *nothing* could block the signal!"

"*I'll* do it," said Gipsy, taking the device from Chas. "I'm the lightest here."

And before anyone could argue, she started to climb up the pile of giraffes.

Abbiz spoke soothingly to the animals and they held very still for her. Some of them even licked Gipsy as she went – they trusted her because she had been kind to them. Up she went, treading as lightly as she could, heading for the very top of the giraffe pyramid.

But the ground was starting to shake as the moon got nearer and nearer. Gipsy struggled to keep her balance as she climbed up onto the back of the highest giraffe.

"Quickly, Gipsy!" Teggs yelled. "Try it now!"

Gipsy switched on the device and wiggled its joystick. "It's no good! It still won't work!"

"Keep trying!" he urged her. "It's our only chance!"

In desperation, Gipsy held the remote high above her head. Teggs gulped. She and the giraffes looked tiny, silhouetted against the great, green moon. Could the extra height she had gained make any difference at all?

YES, IT COULD!

Suddenly, with a sound like the screech of brakes, the mighty wrecking-ball moon stopped in its tracks. It grew no bigger, and the ground stopped shaking.

"It's working!" hooted Gipsy excitedly. "Look, I can steer it! Wheeeee!"

Everyone gasped as the moon started to move about above them – first in a circle, then in a figure of eight.

"Er, very good," Chas called nervously. "But can you press the big blue button? With any luck, that should put the moon into reverse!"

Gipsy did as he asked. "Here goes!"

And with a whooshing, swooshing noise, the moon began to fly away from them. It seemed to grow smaller and smaller as it retreated faster and faster. Then it started to judder and wobble about, like it wasn't sure which way to go.

"It must be getting out of range," murmured Chas. "Our signal and the mammoths' signal are mixing together, and scrambling its circuits."

Suddenly Teggs's communicator beeped. Tonka's voice rang out furiously. "Oi! What d'you think you're doing? Give me my ball back."

Teggs grinned and shook his head. "If you can't play with it nicely, you can't play with it at all!"

"That moon's going mental!" Iggy cried. "Look!"

The bogus moon jerked about like invisible hands were tugging it this way and that.

And then . . . it blew up!

For a moment the whole sky burned brightly. Then a million green fireworks were left hanging in the sky above them, mingling with the stars.

"It worked!" Teggs murmured, barely able to believe it. "It actually worked!"

"We're safe!" whooped Abbiz, bouncing around with glee. "The whole planet is safe again!"

Chas beamed. "We may not have one big moon any more – but we've got hundreds of little ones to make up for it!"

"Well done, Chas!" roared Iggy. "And well done Gipsy and her amazing performing giraffes!"

Everyone clapped and cheered madly. Gipsy jumped down from the top of the pyramid and Teggs made sure he caught her. She gave him a big, happy hug as the giraffes scrambled down from each other's shoulders and took a bow.

But then Tonka's voice crackled over Teggs' communicator. "You will pay for spoiling our plans like this!"bellowed the maddened mammoth. "Now we're going to whizz over and wreck *you* – ARGHHH!"

"I don't think they will!" Arx grinned, holding his own communicator to his ear. "The dimorphodon tell me that a big lump of that exploding moon has crunched into Tonka's flashy spaceship! The mammoths are spinning out of control – and out of this solar system."

"Wrecked by their own wrecking ball," said Teggs happily. "Serves them right!"

"Shame I never got a chance to thank Tonka," said Iggy, much to everyone's surprise. "I won't need the shuttle to take all the triceratops back to their camp any more – now we've landed, they can walk!"

Abbiz smiled. "Thanks to you, we'll soon have this planet up and running," she said. "And then, who knows? Perhaps I'll join the Astrosaurs Academy and go on my own space adventures – just like Uncle Arx!"

"You'll be a star," Teggs predicted.

"Just don't be a moon!" joked Iggy.

"What about the giraffes?" asked Gipsy, looking worried. "What will happen to them now?"

"Don't worry," said Teggs. "Once Iggy has fixed the *Sauropod*, we'll take them somewhere nice and quiet."

"No need," said Chas. "They can stay here on Aggadon as our honoured guests!"

The giraffes did backflips, and then bowed again gratefully.

Teggs grinned. "Well in that case, we'd better take away those performing circus fleas and find *them* a new home. Hey, perhaps I could give them to Admiral Rosso to keep as pets?"

Arx frowned. "Giving fleas to your commanding officer is never a good idea, Captain!"

"Oh? Sounds like fun to me," said Teggs with a naughty smile. "But here's an even better idea – the moment the *Sauropod* is fixed, let's set off on another adventure." He stared up at the starry sky and smiled. "There are a million places to see out there, and I'm *itching* to visit them all!"

THE END

ASTROSAURS
BOOK TEN

THE STAR PIRATES
Read the first chapter here!

Chapter One

INVISIBLE ATTACK

Way out in the dark depths of space, a
stegosaurus and a triceratops were
waiting in a rusty old
spaceship.

Waiting for
someone to attack
them!

"This ship is total
rubbish," declared
Teggs. He tried to sit

in a rusty chair but it broke beneath him and he landed on his bottom. "I never saw such a useless bag of bolts!"

"Me neither," agreed Arx. "The guns don't work, the steering is dodgy, and the engines so weedy we could hardly outrun a space-tortoise."

"True," Teggs agreed with a crooked grin. "It's perfect for our plan!"

"I just hope that plan works," said Arx grimly, checking his space armour. "If it doesn't, we are in big trouble!"

Teggs checked his own battle gear, and looked out the window at the comforting egg-shaped sight of the DSS *Sauropod*. The rest of the crew were still aboard, awaiting their captain's signal.

He spoke into his communicator. "Teggs calling Gipsy. Are you there? Let's run through the plan one more time. It's vital we all know what we are doing here."

Arx cleared his throat. "We are here because several spaceships have disappeared in this sector. They were small ships, carrying cargos of electronic parts. They've never been seen again — but their cargos have turned up on other planets."

"And that can only mean one thing," Gipsy put in. "Those ships were hijacked, their crews kidnapped — and anything valuable on board was sold to the highest bidders."

"It's a terrible business," said Teggs sadly. "And we are going to put a stop to it."

"Yes, sir," said Iggy. "We know that those crooks would never dare take on a ship as big and strong as the *Sauropod*. But if they spy a rusty old cargo ship like the one you and Arx are on, chances are they will pick a fight."

"So – what's the plan, Gipsy?"

"We will hide the *Sauropod* and wait," said Gipsy. "If anyone does attack you, we will zoom out and catch them red-clawed!"

"Very good," said Teggs approvingly.

"Captain!" said Arx. He tapped a grimy computer screen with his biggest horn. "According to these readings, we are moving."

"Iggy," Teggs snapped into his communicator. "Anything on the *Sauropod* scanners?"

"Can't see anything, Captain," Iggy reported. "No black holes or space tunnels in the area."

"Something is definitely pulling us away!" Arx insisted.

Teggs knew Arx was right. He looked

out the window, but there was nothing out there.

He blinked, then gasped.

Mysterious black smoke was swirling round outside . . .

"Iggy!" Teggs shouted. "Gipsy, can you hear me?" But his only reply was crackly static. "Arx, we've lost contact with the *Sauropod*!"

Read the rest of
THE STAR PIRATES
to find out which terrible crooks
have attacked Teggs and Arx!